CONTENTS

Stories retold by Maureen Spurgeon

First published 1995 by Brown Watson
The Old Mill, 76 Fleckney Road,
Kibworth Beauchamp,
Leicestershire, England

Reprinted 1996, 1997, 1999, 2000, 2001, 2003

ISBN: 0-7097-1023-2
©1995 Brown Watson, England

Printed in the E.C.

FAIRY TALE
TREASURY

BOOK THREE

Brown Watson
ENGLAND

Goldilocks
and the
Three Bears

There was once a girl whose hair was so pretty, long, fair and curly, that everyone called her Goldilocks.

Goldilocks and her family lived in a cottage at the edge of a great, big forest, and there was nothing she liked better than going for long walks on her own.

Goldilocks thought she must know every inch of that forest until, one morning, after she had set off a little earlier than usual, she saw something which gave her quite a surprise. . .

It was a little cottage she had
never seen before, with lace
curtains at the windows and
smoke coming out of the chimney.
"Who can live here?" wondered
Goldilocks, going up to the door.

She knocked at the door and waited. There was no answer. She knocked again. Still, no answer.

"Anyone at home?" she called, and knocked again, a little harder this time. The door creaked open.

Goldilocks stepped inside and looked all round such a cosy, little room. A fire burned cheerfully, and on the hob were three bowls of porridge - a big bowl, a smaller bowl, and a tiny, little bowl. . .

"I wonder who lives here?" thought Goldilocks again, never guessing it was the home of three bears - Daddy Bear, Mummy Bear and Baby Bear. She only knew how good that porridge looked on a fresh, spring morning.

She tasted Daddy Bear's porridge. That was too hot. Then, she tried Mummy Bear's porridge. That was too cold. But when she tasted Baby Bear's porridge, it was so good that Goldilocks soon ate it all up!

After eating all that porridge, Goldilocks wanted to sit down. So she tried Daddy Bear's chair. That was too hard. Then she tried Mummy Bear's chair, but that was too soft. Then, she tried Baby Bear's chair. . .

And that was just right! In fact, Goldilocks had never sat in such a comfortable chair! She wriggled and squirmed so much, that, in the end, the chair broke, and Goldilocks fell to the floor!

"Ooh!" she groaned. "I think I'd better go and lie down." So, she went upstairs.

And in the bedroom were three beds - Daddy Bear's bed, Mummy Bear's bed, and Baby Bear's bed. . .

First, she tried Daddy Bear's bed. But that was too hard. Then she tried Mummy Bear's bed. That was too soft. But Baby Bear's bed was so warm and so cosy that Goldilocks snuggled down and was soon fast asleep!

By this time, Daddy Bear, Mummy Bear and Baby Bear were coming back from their walk. They had only gone to the end of the forest path and back - "Just to let the porridge cool down," Mummy Bear had said.

"Who's been eating my porridge?" growled Daddy Bear.

"Who's been eating my porridge?" said Mummy Bear.

"Who's been eating my porridge?" cried Baby Bear. "There's none left!"

"And who's been sitting in my chair?" roared Daddy Bear.

"Who's been sitting in my chair?" cried Mummy Bear.

"Who's been sitting in my chair?" wailed Baby Bear. "It's all broken!"

They went upstairs. "Who's been sleeping in my bed?" said Daddy Bear.

"Who's been sleeping in my bed?" squealed Mummy Bear.

"Who's been sleeping in my bed?" said Baby Bear, with a loud sob.

His cries woke Goldilocks and she sat straight up in bed. She could not believe her eyes when she saw three furry faces looking at her! "B-bears!" she blurted out, very frightened. "Th-three b-bears!"

Had Goldilocks known it, Daddy, Mummy and Baby Bear were gentle, kind bears. When they saw it was only a little girl who had been in their cottage, they were not nearly so angry as they might have been.

But Goldilocks only knew that she had to leave their cottage just as soon as she could. So she let out a scream, the loudest, longest scream she had ever screamed, making the Three Bears jump back at once!

This was Goldilocks' chance!
She flung back the bedclothes
and rushed out of the door and
down the stairs, away back into
the forest before the Three Bears
knew what was happening!

On and on she ran through the forest until she felt she could run no more.

It seemed a long, long time before she reached the path which led to her own home.

And there was her mother,

waiting anxiously at the gate.
Goldilocks was so glad to see
her.

"Where have you been,
Goldilocks?" she cried. "Daddy
was just going out to look for
you!"

And so began the story of Goldilocks and the Three Bears. Her mother could hardly believe it!

"You naughty girl!" she scolded. "Haven't I always told you never to go inside strange places?"

"Goldilocks," said her daddy, "are you sure this tale about The Three Bears isn't an excuse because you do not know the forest as well as you thought?"

"No, Daddy!" cried Goldilocks.

"Here," she went on, taking his hand, "I'll take you to their cottage, myself. Then you'll see."

And she led the way back into the forest without stopping once, seeming sure of every step.

That was the first of many times
Goldilocks went back to the forest.
But, no matter how hard she
searched, she did not find that little
cottage, nor The Three Bears - Daddy
Bear, Mummy Bear and Baby Bear.

Snow White
and the Seven Dwarfs

Long ago, a queen sat sewing at a palace window. Looking out at the white snow drifting against the black window frame, she pricked her finger and three drops of blood fell. "If only, I had a daughter with skin as white as snow, blood-red cheeks and hair as black as the window frame," she sighed, "I would call her Snow White."

Before long, the queen's wish was granted. Everyone celebrated the birth of her baby daughter. And, as the years passed, Snow White became more and more beautiful.

But the happy times were not to last. Suddenly, the good queen became ill and died. Within a year, Snow White's father had taken another wife, as hard-hearted as she was beautiful.

The new queen was also very vain. Her greatest treasure was a magic mirror, and every day she asked it the same question. "Mirror, mirror on the wall, who is the fairest one of all?"

The answer from the magic
mirror was always the same.
"In all the land,
'Tis thou, oh queen!
Thou art the fairest
To be seen!"

Then, one day, the mirror gave
a different answer.
"No maiden was more fair
Than thou!
But Snow White is
The fairest, now!"

The queen flew into a terrible
rage, screaming for a palace
guard.
"Take Snow White into the forest!"
she stormed. "Put her to death!
Then bring me back her heart!"

The guard was shocked. He knew he had to do as the queen said. But, by the time he and Snow White reached the forest, he had made up his mind that he could never do such a wicked deed.

He told her of the danger she was in. "Run away, as far as you can," he begged Snow White, "so the queen will not find you! I shall take back a deer's heart and pretend it is your's!"

Poor Snow White! She would never have thought anyone could hate her so much. On and on she ran, strange shadows looming everywhere, and thorns

and brambles seeming to reach out, clawing at her. How long she kept running, she hardly knew. It seemed like a dream when, quite suddenly, she came across a little cottage nestling in the very heart of the forest.

"Anyone at home?" she called,
stepping inside. How dusty and
untidy it was in that little cottage!
But Snow White was so glad to
have somewhere to rest, she did
not mind.

She set to work, feeling much happier as she laid a fire, ready to cook some broth.

"I wonder who lives here?" she thought, dusting the seven little chairs set around the table.

By the time she had washed seven little plates, seven mugs, seven knives, spoons and forks, then made seven little beds, Snow White was feeling very tired. She only meant to rest a little while . . .

When she woke up, there were the faces of the seven dwarfs smiling at her. How pleased they had been to return to a warm, clean cottage, and find a meal waiting for them, cooked by a pretty girl!

As soon as they heard what had happened to her, the dwarfs said she could stay with them. Snow White had not been so happy for a long time. She loved looking after the seven dwarfs.

"Do not open the door to anyone
while we are out," they told her.
"If ever the queen should hear
where you are, she will surely
try to harm you again." Snow
White knew this was true.

At that very moment, the magic
mirror was telling the queen,
"In the seven dwarfs' cottage,
Snow White lives now.
She is, dear queen,
Still fairer than thou!"

The queen went white with rage! Determined to put an end to Snow White, she disguised herself as an old pedlar woman, then put poison into the rosiest apple she could find . . .

With her magic powers, the queen soon found the cottage in the forest and tapped at the door. "Lovely apples!" she croaked, as Snow White came to the window. "Try one, my dear."

Snow White did not want to hurt
an old woman's feelings. One
bite of the poisoned apple and
she fell to the floor. Cackles of
wild laughter from the wicked
queen echoed all through the
forest.

The dwarfs were heartbroken
when they found dear Snow White.
Wanting to keep her with them
for always, they put her in a
crystal casket and set it down in
her favourite part of the forest.

As time passed, the story of the beautiful young princess asleep in a crystal casket began to spread. One day, a handsome young prince decided to discover the truth for himself.

The moment he saw Snow White, he had to lean over and kiss her. Her eyelids fluttered, and as she looked into the face of the young prince, she knew she loved him as much as he already loved her.

Very soon, the dwarfs were
invited to Snow White's wedding.
Only the wicked queen did not
join in the celebrations. When
she heard the news, she got
into such a temper that she
disappeared in a puff of smoke!

Red Riding Hood

There was once a girl called Little Red Riding Hood. That was not really her name, but her grandmother had made her a red hood and cape, rather like those which ladies wore under their hats when they went out riding. And so, Red Riding Hood was what everyone called her.

Now, Red Riding Hood was a nice little girl, always cheerful and kind. So, when she heard that her Grandma was ill, she asked if there was anything she could do to help.

"Well, Red Riding Hood," said her mother, "I'd be glad if you could take some food to Grandma and see how she is. But it would mean you'd have to go through the wood!"

"Oh, I don't mind!" cried Red Riding Hood. She was thinking how nice it would be to stroll through the wood, and maybe pick some flowers for Grandma on the way.

"Well," said her mother again,
"you must promise to go straight
to her house, and no dawdling!
Remember not to stop and speak
to anyone you don't know!"

Now, Red Riding Hood really did mean to do what she had been told. But it was all too easy to forget, especially with the sun shining and so much to see on the way.

It was all so quiet, she had no
idea that anyone else was there.

"Little Red Riding Hood . . . "
murmured the wolf, seeing the
red cloak. "She'd make a fine
supper . . ."

"Good day, Red Riding Hood," he said with a friendly bow. "May I ask where you are going?"

"To Grandma's cottage," she said. "On the other side of the wood."

This set the wolf thinking.

"Why not take a short cut along this path, my dear?" he said, knowing very well that the way he pointed was twice as long . . .

But his idea was to get to the
cottage long before Red Riding
Hood. Then, he thought, he could
eat up poor Grandma, as well.
What a feast he would have!

Still panting a little, the wolf knocked on Grandma's door.

"Who is there?" she quavered.

"It's me, Grandma," replied the wolf, in a voice as sweet as he could make it. "Red Riding Hood."

"Red Riding Hood!" cried Grandma in delight. "Lift up the latch and come right in."

And, with a loud roar, that wicked wolf burst into the cottage!

Poor Grandma fainted at once, but before the wolf could take the first bite, he heard the sound of a gun outside. Best put the old woman in the wardrobe, he decided.

The sound of guns told the wolf
that hunters were about, and the
wolf did not like hunters one bit!
Besides, he thought, Red Riding
Hood would be arriving soon . . .

So he put on Grandma's nightcap and gown and got into bed. Soon, a voice called, "Grandma! It's Red Riding Hood!"
"Come in, dear!" cried the wolf.

"Oh, Grandma!" exclaimed Red Riding Hood, as she came up to the bed. "What big eyes you have!"

"All the better to see you with!" murmured the wolf.

"But, Grandma!" Little Red Riding Hood said again, "what big ears you have!"

"All the better to hear you with," growled the wolf.

Red Riding Hood began to think that something was very strange . . .

"But, Grandma!" she said for a third time, "what big teeth you have!"

"All the better to EAT you with!" roared the wolf, and he leapt out of bed. He reached out to grab Red Riding Hood with his long, powerful claws!

Red Riding Hood began screaming, which made her Grandma bang on the wardrobe door. The wolf roared again, not knowing that the hunter he had heard was right outside . . .

He kicked the door open and
strode into the cottage, raising his
gun. He had been hunting the
wolf for a long time – as that
cowardly beast knew only too
well!

With one last, desperate roar, he dashed out of the cottage, determined to escape the hunter's gun for the last time. After that, he was never seen again.

By this time, Red Riding Hood had heard the banging on the wardrobe door, and let her Grandma out. And how glad they were to see the last of that wicked wolf!

But, Red Riding Hood began to cry.

"It's my fault," she sobbed. "I should have done what Mummy told me, and not spoken to the wolf."

"Well," smiled Grandma, "I'm sure you won't do it again, dear."

"Now," she went on, "let's all have some tea. Then our friend the hunter can see you safely home."

Stories I have read

Goldilocks and the Three Bears ☑

Red Riding Hood ☑

Snow White and the Seven Dwarfs ☑

The Ugly Duckling ☑

The Wizard of Oz ☑

Pinocchio ☐